To Danica, Sarah, and Josh,

Thank you for the love and enthusiasm you show for our Christmas traditions,
the fun and the laughter that you bring to our Christmas celebrations,
and for the unstoppable excitement that you demonstrate for everything Christmas.

–R.O.

Merry Christmas to Ken, Irene, and all the Hewson kids—
Eric, Colleen, and Jack

–B.D.

The Legend of the
CHRISTMAS
TREE

Written by
Rick Osborne

Illustrated by
Bill Dodge

zonderkidz

Tonight's the night we get our Christmas tree!" Amanda and Beth Johnson sang and squealed.

"Presents, presents, presents," Buddy, their younger brother, chanted.

Mom saw a wrinkled-brow expression on Dad's face that stole part of his smile. "Why is Christmas so much about trees, decorations, and gift getting?" Dad grumbled.

"I like trees…and presents, too," Mom said, trying to iron the creases out of his brow.

"Yeah, I guess," Dad said out loud. But he was thinking, *I would love a Christmas that's more about the manger and its meaning than about spending money.*

"Dinner's ready, kids," Mom called.

A blast of inviting smells, plump with Christmas memories, greeted the children as they thundered into the kitchen and gathered around the table for dinner. Dad began with prayer: "Lord, thank you for providing for us, for all the fun Christmas is, and for this wonderful food. Please help us find ways to make the birth of your Son, Jesus, a bigger part of our celebration." When the prayer was done, the clash and clatter of cutlery against the Christmas dishes rang out as the Johnsons served up their traditional get-the-Christmas-tree-night dinner.

After the family had their fill of meatballs, scalloped potatoes, and sweet baby carrots, Mom pushed back from the table and sounded the battle cry. "Let's get a Christmas tree!"

It didn't take long for five satisfied tummies to find their ten excited feet. Minutes later everyone was snug in warm winter gear and heading outside. Dad pulled the family four-by-four out onto the snow-blanketed road. The annual hunt for the family tree was on.

"Can we get a really big Christmas tree this year?" Amanda, the oldest, asked as she leaned forward in excitement.

Dad's brow started to wrinkle once again. "I don't think we can afford a big one right now, dear."

"Why don't we go to a tree farm and cut our own?" Mom suggested.

"That's a great idea!" Dad agreed.

Twenty minutes later they drove into a thick, soupy fog. It seemed obvious to everyone except Dad that they were lost.

"There it is!" called Buddy. He pointed to a small sign that suddenly appeared out of the foggy night. Dad turned in and bounced slowly down a long, narrow driveway until they came to a clearing where a snack shack and roaring fire welcomed them.

A grandfatherly man dressed in a red flannel shirt, green denim overalls, and large smile gave them an excited wave as if he had been expecting them. As the group trudged into the clearing, they noticed a strange sight. Three large, perfect Christmas trees were set up in beautiful wrought-iron stands. All three were identical in height and shape, but each was decorated differently.

Beneath the last tree sat a lone box. Its silver wrapping paper caught the glimmer of the flickering fire. It almost seemed to glow.

Beth, the second oldest, stared curiously at the trees. "Why do you have those trees set up that way?" she asked.

"What's in the box?" Amanda asked.

"The trees and the secret in the box tell the legend of the Christmas tree," their host explained.

"A legend? Tell us! Tell us!" Buddy pleaded.

The tree farmer looked at Mom and Dad. "Well, I guess we have some time," Mom said. "But first let's get some goodies from the snack shack."

Once everyone had a dark-chocolate brownie in one glove and a tall mug of marshmallow-topped hot cocoa in the other, they followed the farmer to warm log seats by the fire.

With a grin, the farmer wiped his oversized mustache, checking for stray marshmallow, and started his story. "At first, cutting down a small evergreen had nothing to do with Christmas. It started over a thousand years ago when a monk named Boniface used the evergreen tree as a way to tell people about God."

Dad looked up from his hot chocolate. "Really? The Christmas tree told about God?"

"Yes," the storyteller went on. "Boniface explained to the people that just as the tree had three corners but was still one tree, so God is one God who exists in three persons: Father, Son, and Holy Spirit. Soon people who wanted to teach like Boniface were cutting trees and hanging them up in churches. And from there the legend of the Christmas tree began."

The storyteller moved to the first tree. "During the time of knights and castles, people celebrated a special holiday on December twenty-fourth and called it the Feast of Adam and Eve. They decorated evergreen trees with apples and twists of bread to tell the story of the tree in the Garden of Eden."

"I know that story." Buddy had finished his brownie. "Adam and Eve ate some fruit from a tree in the Garden that God told them not to touch. So God sent them out of the Garden."

"But how did the Adam and Eve tree end up being about Jesus' birthday?" Amanda asked as the fire crackled suddenly and the silver box glittered.

The farmer smiled at Amanda and continued. "Well, the story of Adam and Eve bringing sin into the world wasn't complete without the story of Jesus. Over the years people added other kinds of decorations that told the story of Jesus' birth—flowers, fruit, wafers. These decorations stood for other parts of the story of Jesus. But the decorated tree still wasn't a Christmas tree…not yet."

The storyteller then took two giant steps and stood by the second tree.

"A long time ago, before electric lights were invented and after Christmas had been chosen as the day to celebrate Jesus' birth, a church leader named Martin Luther was on his way home after a late Christmas Eve church service. As he walked, he saw starlight reflecting off the icicles that hung from a small evergreen tree."

Dad was listening so carefully that he forgot to drink his hot chocolate. Buddy, always wanting to be helpful, drank it for him.

"Martin Luther cut down that little tree, set it up in his home, and put candles on it. He used it on Christmas day to tell his children the story of the birth of Jesus, who came to die for our sins and become the Light of the world."

The storyteller's big boots moved him beside the third tree.

"Oh, that tree's my favorite," twittered Beth, gaping at all the flickering white lights and the many gorgeous decorations.

"Soon after that, people in Europe began decorating trees for Christmas much as we do today. They decorated with beautiful glass ornaments, trinkets, and tempting treats. This was their way of celebrating Jesus' birth."

"I see," Dad said, lost in thought as he tried to drink from his empty mug. A moment later big, cold snowflakes melting on his face brought him back from his thoughts.

That's the legend of the Christmas tree," the big man said.

"What a cool story!" Amanda said, watching her brother trying to catch a snowflake on his tongue.

"Dad, can we get a tree now?" Buddy asked.

"Yes." Dad's face was decorated with a huge smile. He knew what he was going to do. "Let's get a *big, beautiful* Christmas tree just like one of these." All three children cheered and danced in the snow.

"I have just the one," declared the farmer as he marched over to a large tree leaning against the snack shack.

Mom saw the "reserved" sign the farmer cut off the tree and slipped into his pocket. "But wasn't that tree..."

"Reserved just for you," the storyteller interrupted with a wink.

A short while later, the tree was tied tightly to the top of the four-by-four. Just before they pulled out, the farmer handed Dad the silver, gift-wrapped box. "No shaking or peeking, and don't open it until you've finished decorating your tree." Everyone cheered a chorus of "thank you" as they waved good-bye. The children watched out the frosted back window of the four by four as the jolly tree farmer, still waving, faded into the fog and a curtain of gently falling snow.

The next morning was the last Saturday before Christmas. Outside it was wintry and white. But inside, the smell of pancakes and pine needles filled the warm house.

Amanda helped Dad wrestle the tree into its stand. Beth and Buddy helped in the kitchen and tried to sneak a peek under the tea towels covering two large cookie sheets on the counter. But Mom's smile let the kids know that this was her surprise.

Everyone looked forward to decorating the Christmas tree, but Dad…well…he seemed almost *too* excited. He had been whistling and singing Christmas carols all morning, and he didn't let little things like singing on key or even getting the words right stop him.

"Let's decorate our Christmas tree," Dad half called and half sang as he placed the silvery, glistening box under the tree.

Who remembers what Boniface showed the people of his time with a bare evergreen tree?" Dad asked when everyone stood admiring the tree.

"That just like the tree is one tree and yet has three corners, so God is one God who exists in three persons: Father, Son, and Holy Spirit," Amanda answered quickly.

Now Mom brought the cookie sheets from the kitchen and uncovered her creations made from golden-brown gingerbread shaped as bread twists and apples.

"Could we eat just one?" Beth asked.

"One twist each, but take a lesson from Adam and Eve and stay away from the apples," Mom said, and everyone laughed.

While the Johnson family hung gingerbread-cookie apples and twists, they talked about what had happened in the Garden of Eden. Then as the kids helped Mom string lights around the tree, Dad did what Martin Luther had done long, long ago. He read the story of Jesus' birth. The last thing the family did was to open boxes and dig out their favorite ornaments and hang them on the tree.

The last ornament was barely on the tree when Beth reached for the silver box. "The tree farmer said we could open it now."

"Go ahead, Beth, open it up for us," Mom told her. The whole family huddled around Beth on the floor. When she was done ripping the paper, she reached into the box and carefully pulled out a beautiful glass star.

"Wow, that's stunning!" Mom said, wide-eyed.

"What does the tag say?" Amanda wondered.

Dad, with tears in his eyes, read the handmade note that hung from the star on a delicate silver cord. "Just as the wise men found Jesus under the star of Bethlehem, may all who see the tree that is under *this* star hear and understand the true meaning of Christmas."

Everyone cheered as Dad placed the star on the top of the tree.

Then they stood back and silently stared at the tree. It seemed to all of them that this was the most beautiful tree they had ever had. Dad broke the silence as he wrapped his arms around his family. "I'm glad God gave us trees and decorations and gifts to help us celebrate the true meaning of Christmas."

zonder**kidz**®
The children's group
of Zondervan

www.zonderkidz.com

The Legend of the Christmas Tree

ISBN-10: 0-310-70043-4
ISBN-13: 978-0-310-70043-2

Requests for information should be addressed to:
Zonderkidz, Grand Rapids, Michigan 49530

Editor: Gwen Ellis
Art Direction: Lisa Workman

Printed in China
07 08 /TPC/ 5 4 3